CAREER EXPLORATION

Marine Biologist

by Jennifer Wendt

Consultant:
Dr. Andre M. Landry, Jr.
Department of Marine Biology
Texas A&M University at Galveston

CAPSTONE BOOKS
an imprint of Capstone Press
Mankato, Minnesota

Capstone Books are published by Capstone Press
151 Good Counsel Drive, P.O. Box 669, Mankato, Minnesota 56002
http://www.capstone-press.com

Library of Congress Cataloging-in-Publication Data
Wendt, Jennifer.
    Marine biologist/by Jennifer Wendt
    p.cm.—(Career exploration)
    Includes bibliographical references and index.
    Summary: Introduces the career of marine biologist, discussing educational requirements, duties, workplace, salary, employment outlook, and possible future positions.
    ISBN 0-7368-0330-0
    1. Marine biologists—Juvenile literature. [1. Marine biologists. 2. Vocational guidance. I. Title. II. Series.
QH314.W46 2000
578.77'023—dc21   99-35396
                                                                                    CIP

Editorial Credits
Matt Doeden, editor; Steve Christensen, cover designer; Kia Bielke, illustrator;
    Heidi Schoof, photo researcher

Photo Credits
Index Stock Imagery, 16, 27, 30, 39
International Stock/Steve Lucas, 15; Jeff Rotman, 22
Jay Ireland & Georgienne Bradley, 46
Tom & Therisa Stack/TOM STACK & ASSOCIATES, 24, 40
Visuals Unlimited, 34; Visuals Unlimited/Inga Spence, cover; Daniel W. Gotshalk, 6;
    W.A. Bonaszewski, 9; Marc Epstein, 10; Kjell B. Sandved, 13; Mark
    Newman, 19; Rick Poley, 21; H.W. Robison, 33; Glenn Oliver, 36; Jeanette
    Thomas, 45

Table of Contents

Chapter 1 Marine Biologist 7

Chapter 2 A Day on the job..................... 17

Chapter 3 The Right Candidate............... 25

Chapter 4 Preparing for the Career 31

Chapter 5 The Market 37

Fast Facts 4

Skills Chart..................................... 28

Words to Know................................ 42

To Learn More................................ 43

Useful Addresses 44

Internet Sites................................. 47

Index 48

Fast Facts

Career Title	Marine Biologist
O*NET Number	24308B
DOT Cluster (Dictionary of Occupational Titles)	Professional, technical, and managerial occupations
DOT Number	041.061-022
GOE Number (Guide for Occupational Exploration)	02.02.03
NOC Number (National Occupational Classification-Canada)	2121
Salary Range (U.S. Bureau of Labor Statistics and Human Resources Development Canada, late 1990s figures)	U.S.: $18,700 to $74,000 Canada: $4,500 to $49,800 (Canadian dollars)
Minimum Educational Requirements	U.S.: bachelor of science degree Canada: bachelor of science degree
Certification/Licensing Requirements	U.S.: none Canada: none

Subject Knowledge	Biology; chemistry; English; food production; mathematics; physics; technical writing
Personal Abilities/Skills	Use logic and scientific methods to study living things and their environments; understand and follow instructions; learn and use knowledge about how living things function and how plants and animals are classified; learn how to use scientific equipment; recognize differences in size, form, shape, color, and texture; use hands, eyes, and fingers easily and accurately; make decisions; perform tasks which require great care and accuracy; write up findings of research and make technical presentations
Job Outlook	U.S.: faster than average growth Canada: fair
Personal Interests	Scientific: interest in discovering, collecting, and analyzing information about the natural world and in applying scientific research findings to problems in medicine, life sciences, and natural sciences
Similar Types of Jobs	Aquaculturist; anatomist; biologist; botanist; ecologist; limnologist; microbiologist; physiologist; zoologist

Chapter 1

Marine Biologist

Marine biologists are scientists who study aquatic life. They learn and teach others about plants and animals that live in the world's seas and oceans. These plants and animals are called aquatic life.

Marine biologists sometimes help aquatic animals that are in trouble. They help sick or injured animals get better.

What Marine Biologists Do

Marine biologists study saltwater aquatic life. The world's seas and oceans contain saltwater. Some lakes and rivers contain saltwater. But most lakes and rivers contain freshwater. Freshwater contains little or no salt.

Marine biologists study aquatic habitats. These are the natural places and conditions in

Marine biologists study life that lives underwater.

which plants and animals live. Marine biologists also study ecology. Ecology is the study of the relationships between plants and animals in their environments. Marine biologists learn how plants and animals interact in their habitats.

Some marine biologists do research. Research is the close and careful study of a subject. Marine biologists learn about aquatic life through research.

Marine biologists sometimes use their knowledge to help keep aquatic environments healthy. They do this in many ways. Some marine biologists keep track of fish populations for governments or fishing companies. This helps governments and fishing companies set fishing limits. This is the number of fish individuals and companies can legally catch.

Other marine biologists care for aquatic life at zoos or aquariums. These marine biologists decide which foods animals eat. They also make sure plants and animals live in healthy environments.

Marine biologists may study the contents of a fish's stomach to learn what it eats.

Tools Marine Biologists Use

Computers are one of marine biologists' most important tools. Marine biologists use computers to track information about aquatic plants and animals. They may use computers to communicate with satellites in outer space. These spacecraft orbit the Earth. Marine biologists use sensing equipment on these

satellites. This equipment helps marine biologists track environmental conditions that may affect aquatic plants and animals.

Marine biologists use computers to show others what they have learned. They may create graphs and charts on computers. They also may type reports, newspaper articles, and scientific journal articles about their research. They may use the Internet to communicate with other scientists.

Marine biologists use other tools when they study aquatic life in the field. Marine biologists usually go to the ocean to study in the field. They may use boats and scuba gear to observe aquatic life. Scuba gear allows people to breathe underwater through air tanks. Marine biologists use cameras to take photographs and record videos of aquatic life. They may use nets to collect specimens. Marine biologists closely study these plants and animals.

Marine biologists sometimes use special equipment to study aquatic life from a

A specimen is a plant or animal that marine biologists study closely.

distance. They may use remotely operated vehicles (ROVs) for deep-sea observations. These small craft contain cameras and other sensing equipment. Marine biologists also may place special radio tags on aquatic animals. Marine biologists use satellites to monitor the tags. This helps them learn about animals' patterns of movement in the ocean.

Marine biologists use other tools in their laboratories. They perform much of their research in these rooms. Marine biologists use powerful microscopes to see tiny details of specimens. Marine biologists place living specimens in special tanks called flow chambers. Flow chambers include jets of constantly moving water. Marine biologists can observe how animals swim by placing them in these chambers.

Work Environment
Marine biologists work both indoors and outdoors. They spend much of their time in laboratories. They also may work on boats and along coasts.

Some marine biologists work in laboratories.

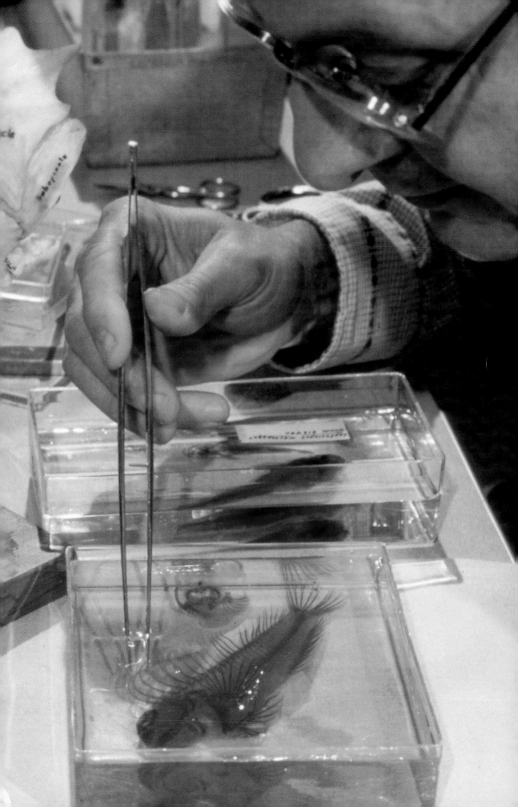

Marine biologists work in a variety of climates. Some work in the warm, calm waters of the Caribbean Sea. Others work in the cold, rough waters of the North Atlantic Ocean.

Marine biologists may work alone or in teams. This depends on the type of research they perform. For example, marine biologists who work on large government projects often work in teams. Marine biologists who work for small companies or universities may work alone.

Marine biologists work many hours when they do research. They may spend days or weeks in the field. They may travel to distant places to study plants or animals.

Some marine biologists are on call. This means they always must be ready to work. Marine biologists at zoos may have to care for sick animals at any time of the day or night. They may have to help marine mammals give birth or care for young.

Scuba

Scuba stands for "self-contained underwater breathing apparatus." Marine biologists use scuba gear to observe aquatic life underwater. Scuba gear includes air tanks, masks, fins, and buoyancy control devices (BCDs). Tanks provide air to divers through breathing tubes. Masks keep water out of divers' eyes and noses. Long, rubber fins help scuba divers swim underwater. BCDs are special devices that help divers rise and sink in the water.

Marine biologists must have special training to scuba dive. They take classes to learn how to operate scuba gear and how to dive safely.

Chapter 2

A Day on the Job

Marine biologists perform different tasks each day. Their tasks and daily schedules depend on the work they perform. Some marine biologists spend most of their time in the field. They study aquatic life along coasts, from boats, and underwater. Some work mostly in laboratories. Others teach in classrooms.

Marine biologists may have many different job titles. These include aquarium keepers, research biologists, and marine mammal trainers. Each job requires different duties.

Aquarium Keepers

Aquarium keepers care for aquatic life at zoos and aquariums. These marine biologists create and maintain environments for plants and animals. They are sometimes called

Some marine biologists teach high school and college classes.

curators. Aquarium keepers make sure the quality of water in tanks is good. They make sure the water is the correct temperature. They control the diets of the animals under their care. They also treat sick plants and animals.

Aquarium keepers begin each day by checking on the plants and animals under their care. They then check water temperatures and tank equipment. Aquarium keepers may clean the tanks. They may have to wear scuba gear and swim in the larger tanks to clean them.

Aquarium keepers also must feed the animals. They may do this after the zoos and aquariums open so the public can watch. Aquarium keepers may explain the different animals' eating habits. They sometimes allow visitors to help feed the animals.

Aquarium keepers are responsible for the health of the animals on display. They may provide medicine or other treatments to sick animals. Aquarium keepers must be ready at all times to provide emergency care to animals.

**Aquarium keepers are responsible for the health of
the animals under their care.**

Research Biologists

Research biologists perform research for
universities, companies, governments, and
other organizations. These marine biologists
work both in laboratories and in the field. They
collect specimens and track aquatic animal
populations.

Many research biologists study the aquatic
food chain. They learn what aquatic animals
eat. This helps them understand how plant

and animal populations are related. For example, a team of marine biologists may try to understand why dolphin populations in a certain area are low. The team may find out which kinds of fish dolphins eat. Team members then can check the number of fish in the area. This will tell them whether dolphins have enough food to survive in the area.

Research biologists also may study the effects of different kinds of pollution on aquatic life. For example, a marine biologist might go to the site of an oil spill. The marine biologist may study how the oil spill affects different forms of aquatic life in the area.

Marine Mammal Trainers

Marine mammal trainers work with marine mammals such as dolphins, whales, walruses, and sea lions. Mammals are warm-blooded animals that breathe air. Trainers teach these animals various behaviors. They may teach the animals to perform tricks. Trainers who work at zoos and aquariums may put on

Research biologists may study sea turtle eggs to track sea turtle populations.

marine mammal shows for the public. For example, a trainer may teach a sea lion to balance a ball on its nose.

Trainers also teach animals behaviors that help protect the animals. For example, a trainer may teach a whale to rest its fin on the edge of a pool. This behavior allows the trainer to inspect the fin for disease or injury.

Trainers are responsible for the health and safety of the animals they train. They keep tanks and other living spaces clean. They feed the animals. Trainers often work nights and weekends. They must be ready at all times to provide emergency care to the animals.

Marine mammal trainers work with animals such as dolphins.

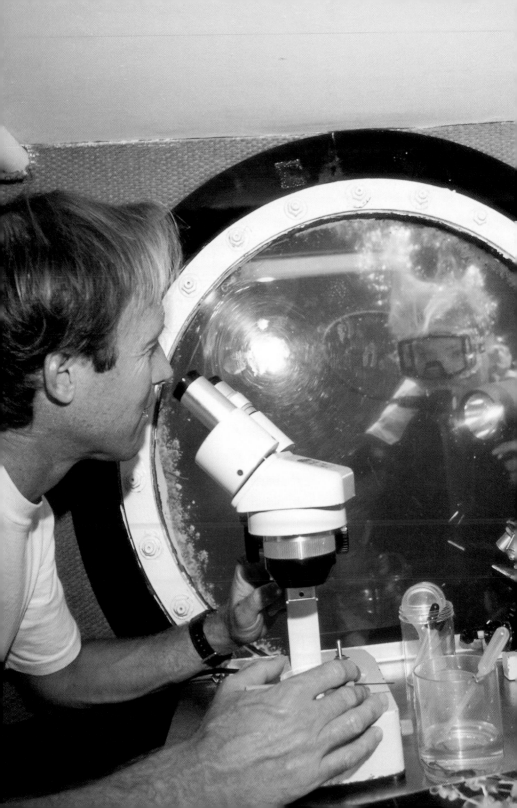

Chapter 3

The Right Candidate

Marine biologists need many skills and abilities to do their jobs. They should enjoy working with and learning about plants and animals. They should enjoy working outdoors. Marine biologists must be able to work independently. They should be comfortable on boats and in the water.

Interests

Marine biologists should be interested in science. Science helps them understand plants, animals, and their environments. Marine biologists also should enjoy working with and learning about nature.

Marine biologists should enjoy sharing information with others. Marine biologists teach others about aquatic life. They may teach

Marine biologists must be able to work on boats and underwater.

classes or write articles for magazines and newspapers. Some work as professors at colleges and universities.

Research biologists should enjoy doing research. They may spend months or years studying the same topics. They should be good at setting and meeting goals. This helps them manage large research projects.

Abilities

Marine biologists must be in good physical condition. They may spend hours walking along coasts, pulling nets, or scuba diving. They may need to lift heavy equipment on and off boats.

Marine biologists should be able to handle rough outdoor conditions. They may have to work on stormy seas or in icy waters. They must be able to perform their duties under many different conditions.

Marine biologists must work well in teams. They should express their ideas clearly to others. They also should be good listeners. This

Marine biologists must be comfortable working outdoors.

helps them understand team members' opinions and suggestions on how to do research.

Skills

Marine biologists must have good water skills. They should be comfortable in the water and on boats. Some marine biologists spend time in the water. These marine biologists should be skilled scuba divers and swimmers.

Skills

Workplace Skills   Yes / No

Resources:
Assign use of time . . . . ✓ ☐
Assign use of money . . . . ✓ ☐
Assign use of material and facility resources . . . . . ✓ ☐
Assign use of human resources . . . . ✓ ☐

Interpersonal Skills:
Take part as a member of a team . . . . ✓ ☐
Teach others . . . . ✓ ☐
Serve clients/customers . . . . ☐ ✓
Show leadership . . . . ✓ ☐
Work with others to arrive at a decision . . . . . . ✓ ☐
Work with a variety of people . . . . ✓ ☐

Information:
Acquire and judge information . . . . ✓ ☐
Understand and follow legal requirements . . . . ✓ ☐
Organize and maintain information . . . . . ✓ ☐
Understand and communicate information . . . . ✓ ☐
Use computers to process information . . . . . ✓ ☐

Systems:
Identify, understand, and work with systems . . . . ✓ ☐
Understand environmental, social, political, economic,
   or business systems . . . . ✓ ☐
Oversee and correct system performance . . . . ✓ ☐
Improve and create systems . . . . ✓ ☐

Technology:
Select technology . . . . ✓ ☐
Apply technology to task . . . . ✓ ☐
Maintain and troubleshoot technology . . . . . . ✓ ☐

Foundation Skills

Basic Skills:
Read . . . . ✓ ☐
Write . . . . ✓ ☐
Do arithmetic and math . . . . ✓ ☐
Speak and listen . . . . ✓ ☐

Thinking Skills:
Learn . . . . ✓ ☐
Reason . . . . ✓ ☐
Think creatively . . . . ✓ ☐
Make decisions . . . . ✓ ☐
Solve problems . . . . ✓ ☐

Personal Qualities:
Take individual responsibility . . . . ✓ ☐
Have self-esteem and self-management . . . . . ✓ ☐
Be sociable . . . . ✓ ☐
Be fair, honest, and sincere . . . . ✓ ☐

Marine biologists must be patient. They must not become bored easily. For example, marine biologists may track fish populations over the course of a year. They must be patient to do these kinds of research tasks.

Marine biologists should be good at math. They use math to keep track of aquatic plant and animal populations. They sometimes create graphs and charts to display the results of their research. Some marine biologists are in charge of budgets. They must plan and record the money they spend.

Research biologists need good research skills. They should read well. They often must read books and magazines about the subjects they research. Research biologists also must have good library skills. This helps them find the books and magazines they need for their research.

Marine biologists need good writing skills. Some marine biologists write reports for companies or government offices. Aquarium keepers may write articles in zoo or aquarium newsletters.

Chapter 4

Preparing for the Career

Marine biologists must earn a bachelor's degree in science. Most students earn this degree in four years. Many marine biologists continue their education after they earn a bachelor's degree. They may earn a master's degree or a doctoral degree.

High School Education

High school students who want to be marine biologists should take science and math classes. Classes that focus on nature are most helpful. These include biology, chemistry, and ecology classes.

Students should take English and speech classes. These classes help students develop

High school students can learn about marine biology on science field trips.

communication skills. Students also should take computer classes to gain computer skills.

Students can benefit by taking part in a variety of activities. They can join swim teams or take scuba lessons. Students also may join science and nature clubs or attend nature camps. They even may serve as camp counselors. Counselors are in charge of younger campers. This helps students gain leadership skills.

Post-Secondary Education

College students who want to be marine biologists should earn a bachelor's degree. They should earn this degree in biology or marine biology. Students should take science classes such as biology, chemistry, ecology, and environmental sciences. Students also may take specialized classes such as fish biology and marine mammalogy. This science is the study of marine mammals.

Additional studies also may benefit college students who want to become marine

Students interested in becoming marine biologists may attend nature camps.

biologists. Students may take additional classes in areas such as computer science, statistics, or mathematics. These classes help graduates find jobs in marine biology.

Continuing Education

Marine biologists continue learning after they earn a bachelor's degree. They study new information and trends in marine biology. Marine biologists may take classes or read professional journals to keep up with the latest research. They also attend science conferences and workshops.

Many marine biologists go back to school to earn a master's degree. Students usually complete this degree in two to three years. Some marine biologists earn a doctoral degree. This is the highest degree offered by a college or university.

Many marine biologists go back to school to earn a master's degree.

Chapter 5

The Market

Marine biologists work in many settings. Their salaries, job outlooks, and opportunities for advancement vary by these work settings.

Salary

Marine biologists' salaries vary. Most marine biologists in the United States earn between $18,700 and $74,000 per year. The average yearly salary is about $28,000. Most marine biologists in Canada earn between $4,500 and $49,800 per year. The average yearly salary is about $29,000.

Marine biologists' salaries depend on their education, experience, and specialty areas. Marine biologists who have a master's degree usually earn more than those who do not.

Marine biologists' salaries depend partly on the kind of work they do.

Those with a doctoral degree usually earn even more. Marine biologists also can increase their salaries by specializing in areas that are in high demand. For example, marine biologists who specialize in computer science may have a greater choice of jobs.

Job Outlook

The job outlook for marine biologists in the United States is good. The number of jobs is expected to grow faster than average. Federal and state governments need more marine biologists to deal with problems such as pollution. Private companies such as fish farms also are hiring more marine biologists.

The job outlook for marine biologists in Canada is fair. Experts expect the number of jobs in the field to stay about the same.

Advancement Opportunities

Marine biologists may advance by taking jobs with more responsibilities. For example, marine biologists who work in teams may gain

Private companies such as fish farms hire marine biologists.

more responsibilities. They may become senior marine biologists. These team leaders are in charge of other team members. Senior marine biologists decide how best to perform research.

Marine biologists often advance by earning higher degrees. Marine biologists who have a doctoral degree usually hold jobs with the most responsibilities. They often serve as senior marine biologists. They help other marine biologists succeed in their areas of study.

Senior marine biologists are team leaders.

Words to Know

biology (bye-OL-uh-jee)—the study of living things

computer science (kuhm-PYOO-tur SYE-uhnss)—the study of computers and how they work

ecology (ee-KOL-uh-jee)—the study of the relationships between plants and animals in their environments

habitat (HAB-uh-tat)—the natural places and conditions in which an animal lives

marine (muh-REEN)—related to the ocean; marine biologists study ocean life and other forms of aquatic life.

microscope (MYE-kruh-skope)—a tool that magnifies very small objects

research (REE-surch)—the close study of a subject

specimen (SPESS-uh-muhn)—a sample that a scientist studies closely

To Learn More

Cosgrove, Holli, ed. *Career Discovery Encyclopedia.* Vol. 5. Chicago: Ferguson Publishing, 2000.

Greenberg, Keith Elliot. *Marine Biologist: Swimming with the Sharks.* Risky Business. Woodbridge, Conn.: Blackbirch Press, 1996.

Hamilton, John. *ECO-Careers: A Guide to Jobs in the Environmental Field.* Target Earth. Edina, Minn.: Abdo & Daughters, 1993.

Higginson, Mel. *Scientists Who Study Ocean Life.* Scientists. Vero Beach, Fla.: Rourke, 1994.

Useful Addresses

American Association for the Advancement
of Science
1200 New York Avenue NW
Washington, DC 20005

International Oceanographic Foundation
Rosenstiel School of Marine and
    Atmospheric Science
4600 Rickenbacker Causeway
Miami, FL 33149-1098

Marine Technology Society
1828 L Street NW
Suite 906
Washington, DC 20036-5104

Vancouver Aquarium Marine Science Centre
P.O. Box 3232
Vancouver, BC V6B 3X8
Canada

Internet Sites

Job Futures—Biology
http://www.hrdc-drhc.gc.ca/JobFutures/english/
   volume2/u620/u620.htm

**Occupational Outlook Handbook—Biological
   and Medical Scientists**
http://www.bls.gov/oco/ocos047.htm

OceanLink
http://oceanlink.island.net/index.html

Secrets of the Ocean Realm
http://www.pbs.org/oceanrealm/seadwellers

Vancouver Aquarium Marine Science Centre
http://www.vanaqua.org/index2.htm

Index

aquarium keepers, 17–18, 29

aquariums, 8, 17, 18, 20

bachelor's degree, 31, 32, 35

chemistry, 31, 32
computer science, 35, 38
curators, 18

doctoral degree, 31, 35, 41

ecology, 8, 31, 32
environmental sciences, 32

flow chambers, 12
food chain, 19
freshwater, 7

Internet, 11

marine mammalogy, 32
marine mammal trainers, 17, 20, 23

master's degree, 31, 35, 37
microscopes, 12

pollution, 20, 38

radio tags, 12
remotely operated vehicles (ROVs), 12
research, 8, 11, 12, 14, 19, 26, 27, 29, 35
research biologists, 17, 19–20, 26, 29

salary, 37–38
saltwater, 7
satellites, 9, 11, 12
scuba gear, 11, 15, 18
senior marine biologists, 41
specimens, 11, 12, 19

workshops, 35

zoos, 8, 14, 17, 18, 20